A B C
Cat

by Nancy Jewell

pictures by
Ann Schweninger

Harper & Row, Publishers

ABC Cat
Text copyright © 1983 by Nancy Bronson Jewell
Illustrations copyright © 1983 by Ann Schweninger

LIBRARY OF CONGRESS CATALOGING IN PUBLICATION DATA
Jewell, Nancy.
    ABC cat.

    Summary: A cat's antics throughout the day take him
through the alphabet.
    [1. Alphabet.   2. Cats—Fiction]   I. Schweninger, Ann,
ill.   II. Title.   III. Title: A B C cat.
PZ7.J55325Ab 1983   [E]   82-48840
ISBN 0-06-022847-4
ISBN 0-06-022848-2 (lib. bdg.)

For Deekis and Rosie—
whose mischief inspired
this story!

Awake, little cat,
take a long stretch,
and arch your back.

Blink at the boy
who's still in bed.
Butt him softly
with your head.

Chowtime, cat!
Click, click, click
on quick cat claws.

Chomp, chomp, chomp
go little cat jaws.

Down, cat, down!

Don't, cat, don't!

Emerald eyes
peer over the shelf
watching the fall
of the china elf.

Funny cat,
foolish cat.
Furry cat,
friendly cat.

Go, cat, go!
Get that puffball under the bed.
Grab that tassel on the spread.

Hurrying here, hurrying there.
Hiding and seeking everywhere.

I see you, cat!

Jump into my lap.

Kiss me, cat!
No time for that?

K nead, knead, knead
and knead some more.

L<small>ICK</small>, lick, lick
your snow-white paw.

Maybe he will
and maybe he won't.

Nosey cat
needs to know everything!

Open the door?
Oh, I see, cat,
it's a…

Paper bag
to poke and pull
and pounce upon.

Quick and quiet
quilt-stalking cat

Rolls himself
right along the rug,

then rolls over
for a belly rub.

Sleepy cat stretched out on the sill.
Statue cat stiller than still.

Tail and eyelids
don't even twitch

Until...

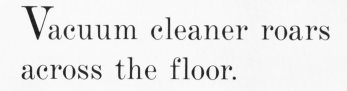

Vacuum cleaner roars
across the floor.

Wide-eyed cat
watches and waits
and then escapes.

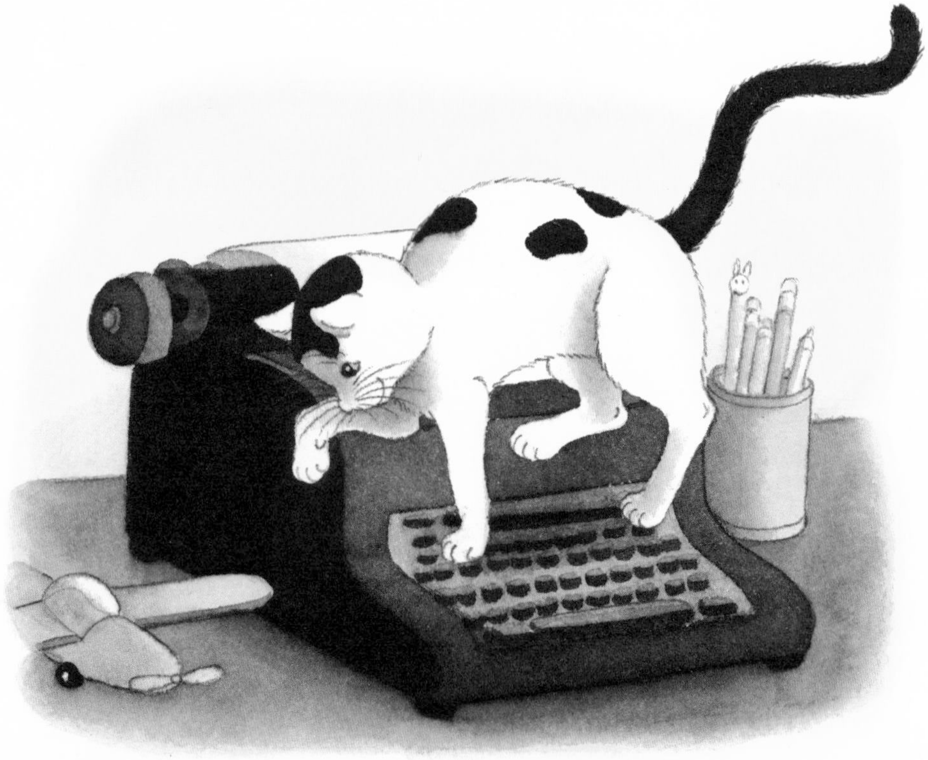

Xxx all over the page.

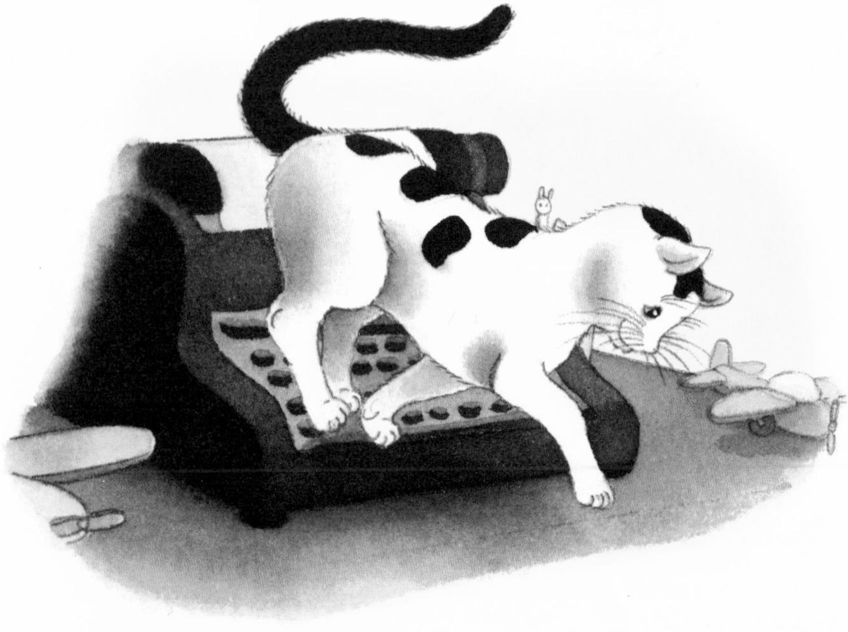

You are some cat!

Zap!